KT-497-891

For Albie
love Mummy
x x x

First published in the UK in 2018 by Nosy Crow Ltd
The Crow's Nest, 14 Baden Place, Crosby Row,
London, SE1 1YW, UK

Nosy Crow and associated logos are trademarks and/or registered
trademarks of Nosy Crow Ltd

Text copyright © Pamela Butchart, 2018
Cover and illustrations copyright © Thomas Flintham, 2018

1 3 5 7 9 10 8 6 4 2

A CIP catalogue record for this book will be available from the British Library.

Printed and bound in Great Britain by
Clays Ltd, Elcograf S.p.A.

Papers used by Nosy Crow are made from wood grown in
sustainable forests.

ISBN: 978 1 78800 116 8

www.nosycrow.com

THERE'S A YETI IN THE PLAYGROUND!

PAMELA
BUTCHART

nosy
crow

Look out for:

BABY ALIENS GOT MY TEACHER!

THE SPY WHO LOVED SCHOOL DINNERS

MY HEADTEACHER IS A VAMPIRE RAT!

ATTACK OF THE DEMON DINNER LADIES

TO WEE OR NOT TO WEE!

THERE'S A WEREWOLF IN MY TENT!

THE PHANTOM LOLLIPOP MAN!

Contents

The Police
AND the
Fire Brigade

For once in my life I wish my mum would understand just how DANGEROUS it is at my school and not say things to me like, "Stop telling tales" or "Don't EXAGGERATE, Izzy" or "Are you SURE the police AND the fire brigade had to come?"

Zach (that's my friend) says that our school is a

DISASTER ZONE

and I think he's right because that's EXACTLY what the fireman said when Gary Petrie got stuck inside the recycling bins again.

And one time after the whole DEMON DINNER LADIES thing, our friend Maisie actually filled in an application to transfer to another school and we had to stop her from posting it because we wanted her to stay with us and also because Jodi says there is

STRENGTH IN NUMBERS (which means it's better to have four of us and not three of us when all the weird stuff starts happening and we have to save the whole school).

But one of the WORST things that's ever happened to us was when it started snowing and it wouldn't stop.

Zach says that we should have DEFINITELY STAYED INDOORS when we heard the

WEIRD
WAILING SOUND

in the playground. And he was right because

if we had then Maisie probably wouldn't have been swept away by the TORNADO.

And even though all the teachers kept telling us that everything was COMPLETELY FINE we all knew that it was COMPLETELY NOT FINE. And in fact that it was probably the most COMPLETELY OPPOSITE OF FINE that you can get because we knew that there was a BEAST on the way to our school.

And we had NO IDEA how to stop it!

Snow Day

Loads of stuff stresses my mum out. Like when she's making tea and I need to be in the kitchen looking for my swimming goggles. Or when Gran says, "When was the last time you dusted in here?" Or when my dad uses the toilet for almost an hour when Mum has guests coming.

But the thing that stresses my mum out the MOST is when it starts snowing. And last week as soon as she saw a TINY SPECK of snow she started

FREAKING OUT

and trying to phone the school and she kept pacing up and down the hall saying, "Come on. Answer. Answer. ANSWER!" And I had to shout that I was TRYING TO SLEEP ACTUALLY because it was 7.23am and I do not have to get up until 7.30am.

And that's when someone started **BANGING** on our front door and Mum shouted, "Izzy! You'll have to get that. I'm on the phone!"

So I got up and I was sure that it must be some sort of

SERIOUS EMERGENCY

because I didn't know who would be banging on the door as loud or as **MUCH** as that at 7.23am except for a police officer or a fire fighter or maybe the Queen. But when I opened the door I saw that it wasn't any

of those people because it was Zach's mum who lives in the flat below us.

At first I thought there was maybe something wrong with Zach or his cat or something because Zach's mum looked PANICKED.

But then she said, "Do we know yet? DO WE KNOW?!"

And my mum shouted down the hall, "I can't get through to the school. The line's been engaged for the past hour. I've left six messages."

I had NO IDEA why my mum was getting so stressed about the school not being open

because of the snow because all it meant was that she'd get to spend the whole day with me because she doesn't even work on a Friday!

So anyway, then the phone rang and Zach's mum screamed, "ANSWER IT!" and then I heard my mum say hello in her PHONE VOICE (which is a lot more posh than her normal voice) and then she said "THANK GOD!" and hung up and started laughing loads and said that the school was open because the snow was forecast to stop at 10am. And then Zach's mum started smiling and laughing loads too and then they hugged each other which I thought was a bit

DRAMATIC

because it was only snow!

Mum and Dad are ALWAYS saying that I am too

DRAMATIC

but I don't almost cry and hug Jodi because of a bit of snow!

So anyway, me and Zach went to school

just like normal and when we got there Jodi was kneeling on the ground measuring the snow with her ruler and Maisie was just standing next to her trying to breathe because she had four coats on and we could only see a tiny bit of her face.

And we all knew that Maisie was wearing so many layers because Maisie's mum is VERY PROTECTIVE of her and she worries about Maisie so much that she does things like make sure Maisie has five extra pairs of gloves with her when it's cold and covers her in sun cream when it's only a TINY bit sunny and sleeps in her car outside my house when Maisie is at a sleepover.

It looked like Maisie was trying to say something so I unzipped her coat a bit so we could see her mouth and that's when she said, "I can't feel my feet."

At first I thought she might have FROST

BITE, which is when your feet get so cold that sometimes one of your toes falls off. But then I realised that it was probably because she was wearing these weird snow boots that looked like they were made out of ANIMAL SKINS and I think I saw an explorer man wearing them in a photo I saw once about Antarctica.

So I tried to loosen the laces because they looked a bit tight, but Jodi said that Maisie's mum must have done a special ARMY KNOT or something because none of us could untie them and Jodi said that we might need to get the school nurse to

CUT the boots off because she was worried about Maisie's BLOOD FLOW. But then everyone forgot about Maisie's furry boots, even Maisie, because Mrs Seith (the scary deputy head) stuck her head out of her office window and shouted at everyone to get up off the ground because all the Year 3s were lying on the ground trying to make SNOW ANGELS.

Then Jodi said that the snow was only ONE CENTIMETRE DEEP which isn't very deep at all, so we all knew that the school wouldn't get closed. But Gary Petrie was still running around telling everyone that it was

"DEFINITELY GOING TO HAPPEN, PEOPLE!"

Then when the bell went, loads of people ignored it because they were too busy trying to scrape enough snow off the ground to make snowballs, so Mrs Kidd (the evil playground monitor) had to blow her whistle three times to get everyone in line.

But when we got to class the snow started coming down a bit harder and Miss Jones (that's our teacher) could barely concentrate on doing the register and she called out

Andrew Cunningham's name

THREE TIMES

because she was too busy STARING out
the window at the snow.

That's when Maisie stared to panic and
said that she just KNEW we were all going
to get SNOWED IN and I had to hold
both her hands and do the BREATHING
EXERCISES her mum showed us how to do
to try to stop Maisie from fainting. But most
of the time it doesn't work and Maisie faints
anyway because Maisie is TERRIFIED of

most things, like buses and pigeons and shepherd's pie.

But then someone knocked on the classroom door and we all looked through the glass window bit and saw that it was one of the office ladies. Everyone held their breath because we all knew that when it's snowing outside and an office lady comes to the door it means that the school is going to CLOSE EARLY.

Miss Jones got up so quickly her chair fell backwards on to the floor. And then she practically RAN to the door. And when she opened it, the office lady actually SMILED at her (and the office ladies NEVER smile).

We all watched with

WIDE EYES

as she handed Miss Jones a slip of paper.

And Jodi said, "We're going to get an **EXTRA LONG WEEKEND!**"

But then Zach said that maybe it **WASN'T** going to be about the snow and that maybe it was about something else, like a school talent show or a trip to Africa or another announcement about the recycling bins and how **UNDER NO CIRCUMSTANCES** are you allowed to play hide-and-seek inside them and that the fire brigade had given the school a **FINAL WARNING** about it.

But when we saw Miss Jones look at the slip of paper we all knew that it **WAS** an

announcement about the snow because she had a HUGE smile on her face. And she looked even more excited than the time parents evening got cancelled because of the GYM HALL ANTS.

As soon as Miss Jones read the line, "Due to worsening weather conditions, the buses will cease operations at 12pm..." everyone GASPED because we knew FOR SURE that the school was

OFFICIALLY CLOSING EARLY!

The BIGGEST Snowman in the World!

As soon as the office lady left, Miss Jones switched off her computer and started packing up her things.

Then she said, "You can all have an **EXTENDED BREAK** in the classroom until school closes at 10.30am." We all looked at

the classroom clock and GASPED because it was only 9.30am which meant we were about to have the

BIGGEST
BREAK EVER!

Gary Petrie put on his jacket and asked if we could go outside but Miss Jones said no because of the snow. But then after ten minutes of us all having the extended break in the classroom she said that she'd changed her mind (even though the snow was coming down much harder than it was when Gary had asked).

So we all started putting on our coats and gloves but Maisie said that there was **NO WAY** she was going out in a **BLIZZARD**. But then Nola Burke started telling everyone that she was going to make the

and that it would get put in the Guinness book of World Records. And that's when Maisie said that she WOULD come and we all knew that it was because Maisie is OBSESSED with the Guinness book of World Records. And one time she tried to eat a

WHOLE
VICTORIA
SPONGE CAKE

in less than TEN SECONDS because she wanted to break the record. But then she started to choke a bit so Jodi had to do the

HEIMLICH MANOEUVRE which is when you hold and squeeze someone in a certain way so that they don't choke to death on any cakes.

So anyway, as soon as we walked outside we all saw that the snow was even HEAVIER than it had been when we left the classroom and it was getting in my eyes a bit.

I was about to say that maybe we should go back inside and get our swimming goggles or something when Zach said, "Over there!" and pointed to the old bike shed and I saw Finola Burke and Roz Morgan rolling a

ball of snow.

Maisie's eyes went HUGE.

And she said, "That must be the HEAD!"

I was a bit shocked when she said that and I said, "If THAT'S the head, how big is the BODY?!"

But Maisie didn't get a chance to answer because all of a sudden the snow got MUCH WORSE and we heard Mr Graves, the head teacher, shouting,

"COME BACK INSIDE!
COME BACK INSIDE!
HURRY!"

Mr Graves wouldn't stop blowing his whistle over and over but we had no idea where he was or which way the school was because the snow had got so bad it was difficult to see.

That's when Jodi shouted,

"HOLD HANDS AND FOLLOW THE NOISE!"

So I grabbed Maisie's hand and Zach grabbed my hand and even though we could hardly see in front of our faces we managed to do what Jodi had said and follow the noise until we eventually got to the Big Doors that led back into school.

As soon as we got inside I saw the LOOK

on Mr Graves's face. And Jodi must have noticed it too because she looked at me with her **WIDE EYES**.

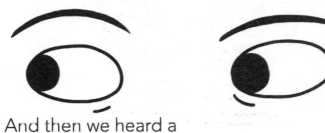

And then we heard a

and we looked down and saw that Maisie had seen Mr Graves's face too because she had fainted right on his feet.

Emergency Assembly

As soon as we got back to the classroom we all noticed that Miss Jones was being a bit weird. She was just standing at the window **STARING** out at the snow with a strange look on her face and she hadn't even asked how Maisie was even though Maisie was wrapped in a blanket, shaking.

That's when Jodi whispered, "That's the EXACT same look Mr Graves had on his face."

And I saw that she was RIGHT.

Then Zach said, "But Miss Jones was so happy before. What happened?"

And Jodi said, "The BLIZZARD happened." But she said it a bit too loudly and Maisie started to shudder VIOLENTLY so I had to shake a pencil case in front of her face to distract her, just like I do with my cats, because she was freaking out.

But Zach said that he didn't think the

BLIZZARD was the reason Mr Graves and Miss Jones looked so worried because we were all safe and no one had fallen over or got lost in a snowdrift or anything like that and that it had to be SOMETHING ELSE that was making them look the way they were looking.

Something BIG.

And as SOON as Zach said that we heard four short bells ring. And I looked at Jodi and she looked at me because we knew that four short bells meant the WHOLE SCHOOL was being called to an

EMERGENCY ASSEMBLY.

And that had only happened two times so far this year: the time when we got told inspectors were coming to our school and the time Mr Graves lost his car keys.

That's when Zach's mouth fell open and he said, "I was RIGHT. It's something BIGGER THAN ALL OF US."

And we had no idea if Zach was right or not. But there was only one way to find out. So I said, "Let's go."

We had to stay in to the left a lot more than we usually do when we go down to the assembly hall because loads of people were rushing past us and most of them were teachers!

I looked down at Maisie to make sure she was OK because Maisie DOES NOT take bad news very well and it was pretty obvious that whatever we were being called to the emergency assembly for WASN'T going to be a good thing.

Then Jodi nudged me and pointed out the window and that's when I saw that the snow was MUCH worse and I couldn't even really see the cars in the car park any more!

When we got to the assembly hall, all the teachers left their classes and stood at the side whispering to each other and they all looked MEGA WORRIED.

Then the scary deputy head walked

on stage and said, "Attention, please."

But all the teachers were too busy being gossipy and they didn't hear her so Mrs Seith said, "AHEM!" really loud into the microphone and then did her WIDE EYES at the teachers and they all stopped whispering and looked down at the ground.

I knew the SECOND that Mrs Seith walked on stage that this wasn't going to be an easy assembly because Mrs Seith uses loads of complicated words that none of us understand and then she says, "Do you all understand? Hmmm??"

And we all just nod and say, "Y-e-s, M-r-s

S-e-i-t-h" even though we have

NO IDEA

what she's talking about.

So we all sat in silence and waited to hear what the emergency assembly was about and that's when Mrs Seith said, "We are currently unable to offer safe exit from the school premises or indeed even to accommodate student access to the school grounds due to the current and impending weather conditions. Therefore, the school building will remain open and in session for the FORESEEABLE FUTURE. Parents have been informed."

And that's when all the teachers GASPED. But none of the pupils gasped because we didn't really know what Mrs Seith had just said.

But then Gary Petrie put his hand up and asked what THE FORESEEABLE FUTURE meant and the deputy head said that it meant

INDEFINITELY.

So then Gary Petrie put his hand up again

and asked what

INDEFINITELY

meant and the deputy head sighed and said that she didn't know how to make it any clearer. So Gary Petrie put his hand up AGAIN and asked if the school was still shutting at 10.30am and Mrs Seith sighed a really long sigh and said, "NO" and that was much easier to understand.

Then one of the Year 6s shouted out, "Are we snowed in?" and Mrs Seith said, "THERE WILL BE NO SHOUTING OUT AT MY

ASSEMBLY." But she didn't answer the question. So then EVERYONE put their hands up and Mrs Seith must have known that we were all going to ask the same question because she did her BIG NOSTRIL thing which is when she shuts her eyes and breathes in really deeply and her nostrils get HUGE.

And then she said, "I suppose you could say that we are snowed in, yes." And that's when everyone GASPED and some of the Year 6 girls started screaming a bit.

Then Mr Graves sort of RAN on to the stage and tried to take the microphone from Mrs Seith (which she didn't look very pleased about).

So he said, "Thank you, Mrs Seith."

And he smiled at her until she eventually took her fingers off the mic and walked off.

And that's when he said, "I'd just like to add a few words and say that we are NOT

snowed in. Yet. A snow storm is headed this way and things are looking quite bad out there but you are all perfectly safe INSIDE the school. So please

STAY INSIDE
THE SCHOOL.

"We can't get you home safely at the minute but we're working on it. Lessons will continue as normal until it's safe to leave."

Then the Year 6 girls started screaming a bit more.

But Zach said, "I can't believe there's a SNOW STORM headed this way. We ARE going to get snowed in! I can't believe it!"

And Jodi got a really serious look on her face and she said, "Maisie, what does

mean?"

So Maisie said that

meant that something could go on and

on and you didn't know when it would stop going on.

And Jodi said, "Wait. Are you saying we might have to stay at school all day and ALL NIGHT??"

And Maisie gulped and nodded.

Starvation, Frostbite and Toilet Water

When we got back to class, **NO ONE** was excited like they were when we thought we were getting to go home early and **EVERYONE** was asking Miss Jones loads of questions about the **SNOW STORM** and getting **SNOWED IN**. But Miss Jones didn't answer ANY of them. She just sat in her chair, staring out of the window at the snow. And she looked MISERABLE.

Jodi said that, based on how worried all the teachers looked and how HEAVY the snow was getting, we needed to make a

SURVIVAL PLAN
ASAP.

And then she said that we needed to FACE FACTS and that the facts were that we might get snowed in OVERNIGHT!

Zach said, "AWESOME!"

And Jodi whipped her head round to face him so fast that Maisie actually jumped out of her seat and landed on the floor next to my feet.

And then Jodi said, "Getting snowed in is

awesome! DO you think STARVATION

is awesome? Hmm? Or FROSTBITE? Or

having to drink TOILET WATER if the

pipes freeze?!"

Zach didn't say anything back because it

was obvious from the way Jodi was speaking

that she was asking RHETORICAL

QUESTIONS (which are questions that you

ask someone when you are annoyed at them

and if they answer them it makes it worse).

Jodi always needs a survival plan when we do most things and she's been like that ever since she watched the whole first season of

EXTREME SURVIVAL

with her mum's new boyfriend.

Not many Year 4s are trained in

EXTREME SURVIVAL.

But Jodi is. And we are thankful for that EVERY DAY, especially when stuff like

THIS happens or like the time on the school camping trip with the

GIANT
WEREWOLF POO.

So Jodi said it was time to talk about RATIONING and that that meant we had to put all of our food together and only let each other eat TINY AMOUNTS to make it last in case we got snowed in overnight, or for the weekend, or EVEN FOR FIVE

MONTHS. That was how SERIOUS the situation was.

That's when Maisie started emptying all the food out of her bag on to the table and I couldn't BELIEVE how many snacks she had in there!

But then Jodi said, "NO! Not here. It's not safe," and she started scooping all the snacks back into Maisie's bag and looking over her shoulder loads while she was doing it.

Jodi said that we couldn't let the rest of the class OR Miss Jones see how much food we had because they might try to STEAL

IT when their food ran out and that it was EVERY MAN FOR THEMSELVES and that we should TRUST NO ONE, not even Miss Jones.

Then Jodi started talking REALLY FAST about water freezing in the pipes and frostbite and then she said that one of us should be taking NOTES because this was SERIOUS and she looked at me when she said it and I got a bit annoyed because we don't usually take notes unless it's an OFFICIAL MEETING and nobody had actually said that it was and we usually only have official meetings in The Den or at one of our houses.

But I was just about to get my pad out of my bag anyway because I knew there was no point in arguing with Jodi when she had

THAT LOOK

in her eye that meant she was IN THE ZONE and that NOTHING could stop her from talking about

SURVIVAL STUFF.

But I was wrong.

Something DID stop her.

Suddenly, Jodi stopped talking MID-SENTENCE and afterwards she couldn't even remember what she had been saying! She was STARING out the window at something and her eyes were SUPER WIDE and she'd gone COMPLETELY PALE.

And then she said, "Is that a snowman and did it just MOVE?!"

Zach JUMPED out of his seat and ran over to the window. But there was nothing there. And then he gave me a look and I knew what he was thinking because I was thinking the same thing. The stress of having to make a

SURVIVAL PLAN

was making Jodi **SEE THINGS**. Like the time she got so stressed about Sports Day and coming **FIRST** in the Whole School Race. I don't think she actually slept for a **WEEK** because when her mum thought she was in bed she was actually in the living room on her mum's exercise bike. But then on the day of

the Sports Day Jodi didn't come first. And she didn't even come second or third or even TENTH. Because she was so tired and STRESSED that she thought she saw a GOAT at the lemonade stand and Miss Jones made her go and have a lie down in the nurse's room.

So anyway, I got up and looked out the window just to be sure because sometimes Zach misses things. But I couldn't see a moving snowman, either. But I DID see that the snow was getting even HEAVIER.

So we told Jodi that we couldn't see the snowman. But we didn't mention the whole

GOAT THING because she gets really annoyed when you bring it up.

And Jodi said, "Oh," and Maisie smiled and gave Jodi a Twix because Maisie always has a spare Twix in her bag and Jodi just took it and said thanks.

That's when someone knocked on the door and we all looked and saw it was Mr Beattie (the new Year 1 teacher) and he looked a bit like he'd been crying.

Miss Jones and Mr Beattie started WHISPERING about something so we waited until Jodi gave the signal and then Zach stood up and walked over to the bin

and pretended to sharpen his pencil so he could get close and hear what was being said.

But when he came back he said that he heard Mr Beattie say "COMPLETELY RUINED" and "DISASTER" and "WORST DAY OF MY LIFE."

And when we looked over at Miss Jones and Mr Beattie, we saw that Mr Beattie was crying a bit and Miss Jones was patting him on the back and saying, "It's going to be all right. We'll survive this. We just have to be STRONG."

And that's when we knew Zach was right.

Something else **WAS** going on.

Something the teachers didn't want us to know about.

And it was definitely

BIGGER THAN ALL OF US.

The Giant Can of Out-of-Date Beans

On our way to dinners, we passed more teachers and they all looked just as upset as Miss Jones and Mr Beattie did and I even saw Mrs Leppard wipe her eyes when she passed us in the corridor.

And it took AGES to get to the dinner

hall because everyone kept stopping and looking out of the windows at the SNOW STORM because the snow was

MEGA HEAVY

and the sky was REALLY DARK and it looked like something out of a FILM.

When we arrived at dinners we all saw that the dinner ladies still had their shutters down and NO ONE knew what was going on, not even the teachers!

Jodi looked at Zach and said, "See? I TOLD you getting snowed in wasn't

AWESOME!"

Maisie said that she didn't want to die of **STARVATION** and her eyes started to go all **SWIRLY** like they do before she faints so we sat down at our table and watched the teachers try to figure out what to do next.

And it was obvious that they were trying to decide **WHO** should be the one to go into the kitchen and ask the dinner ladies where the lunch was and that **NONE** of them wanted to do it because the dinner ladies are even **SCARIER** than the office ladies!

Then eventually we all heard Mr Killington say, "**FINE!**" and he knocked on the kitchen doors and went inside.

We all **STARED** at the doors to see what was going to happen and Zach said that we might actually see Mr Killington **GET THROWN OUT** because the dinner ladies do **NOT** like anyone going back there.

But then we heard a LOUD RATTLING sound and one of the shutters came up and we saw Mr Killington standing there and he was wearing a DINNER LADY APRON and holding a giant can of BEANS.

And he shouted, "OK, everyone. I hope you like BEANS!" and he started opening the giant can and pouring it into a big pot.

We all

GASPED

because we knew that meant that there weren't any REAL DINNERS and also that we were all getting JUST BEANS.

Then Mr Graves rushed into the dining hall and he looked PANICKED and his hair was ALL OVER THE PLACE like he'd been RUNNING. But then he saw Mr Killington with the beans and he said, "THANK GOODNESS," and he calmed down a bit.

Then Mr Graves went over to where all the teachers were standing and started WHISPERING something to them. So Jodi nudged Zach, and Zach got up and wandered over so he could EAVESDROP on what was being said again.

We all watched as Zach pretended that he

was reading the menu on the wall for ages,
even though it was from yesterday, and then
he walked past the teachers

REEEEEEALLY
SLOOOOOOWLY

and came back to the table. And I knew by the
look on his face that he'd heard something

BIG.

Zach said, "Mr Graves just said that the
van that was meant to deliver our lunch got

stuck in the snow! And that the dinner ladies
WERE IN IT!"

And we

GASPED!

Then Mr Graves said, "ATTENTION,
EVERYONE!"

And that's when he told us that we wouldn't
be able to have regular school dinners due
to a "SMALL ISSUE" but that there were
PLENTY of beans to go round and that we
should "TUCK IN".

EVERYONE started moaning about the

BEANS but Jodi said that beans were PERFECT because they are full of PROTEIN which is what we were going to need to STAY STRONG in case we got snowed in for WEEKS.

So Jodi rushed up to get the beans and then

she made us all have SECONDS and she even went up for THIRDS AND FOURTHS!

Loads of people weren't eating their beans and Jodi said that they'd REGRET IT when they realised it was the last meal they'd have for the

FORESEEABLE FUTURE.

But then Maisie said that her tummy felt funny and that she didn't like the beans and that she was worried that the giant can had been OUT OF DATE. And Zach GASPED and said that it might even have been from THE WAR when people had to eat things like that every day.

Jodi's face went a funny shape when Zach said that and we all knew that it was because she'd eaten LOADS of the WAR BEANS.

So I told Jodi that even IF the giant can of beans was out of date that she would probably be FINE because they'd tasted OK and also because my gran says that dates on food aren't actually REAL and that the supermarkets just do that to make you buy more. And Jodi did a little nod so I knew that she was feeling better about it.

Then Maisie said, "Look!" and she pointed to the Glass Doors that go out to the playground and we could all see that the snow was at least KNEE DEEP and there were big piles of it in places where the wind was blowing it.

And that's when Jodi said, "We need to get to The Den.

As soon as we got to The Den, which is our secret place under the stairs that go up to

the boys' toilets, Jodi looked both ways to make sure no one had followed us and then she reached into her pocket and took out the KEY.

Jodi is the only one who is allowed to keep the key because she says that it is a MASSIVE RESPONSIBILITY and that she is the only person she trusts ONE HUNDRED PER CENT not to lose it.

But I always argue with her about that because I only lost the key ONCE and that was ages ago and I was actually the one who found it inside my old trainer at the bottom of my gym bag.

So anyway, as soon as we got inside, we sat down on our buckets and Jodi took out the little whiteboard and pens that we use for our secret meetings and Zach said that he would make some tea because we have

cups and a little sink and a box of teabags in there that the old janitor left behind when he retired. We don't have a kettle, though, so we just use cold water from the tap because none of us really likes tea and we don't have any milk.

So anyway, that's when Jodi said that we needed to know where our next meal was coming from and that it was time to do the FOOD RATIONING because there probably wasn't another giant can of beans in the kitchen.

Maisie emptied her snacks again and she kept opening little zips and flaps and secret

compartments and saying, "Oh. And I've got this too. And this. And this."

And we all knew that it was because Maisie's mum gets

that Maisie is going to get hungry.

But I didn't have any snacks with me that day because Dad had eaten all the fruit and the granola bars and the EMERGENCY

MARS BAR that Mum keeps hidden in the gravy jug in the cupboard that she doesn't think me or Dad know about but we do. So Dad had just given me a pound and said to get something from the tuck shop and not to tell Mum about the MARS BAR.

So I wasn't sure if I was going to have to be the one to

STARVE

to death if we didn't have enough food for all four of us but then Maisie must have noticed that I was worried because she said that we should share everything EQUALLY.

But then Jodi said that even with Maisie's snacks she didn't think we had enough to make it through the night and that

DESPERATE TIMES
CALLED FOR
DESPERATE MEASURES

and we might have to break into the school tuck shop if things got really bad.

And that's when Zach GRABBED a biscuit

and ate it really fast before Jodi could say anything and when he finished Jodi looked FURIOUS but Zach just said that he was sorry and that he couldn't help it because he felt like he had already BEGUN TO STARVE.

Jodi put everything in a plastic bag and wrote POISON on it with a Sharpie pen and drew a little skull and cross bones. Then she said that it was because people might get so hungry that they started trying to STEAL everyone else's food. Zach asked her where she was going to hide the bag but Jodi didn't answer and we all knew that it was because she didn't want him to know after the BISCUIT THING.

That's when Jodi started talking about the snow storm and how we needed to take matters into our OWN HANDS. And then

she said that if the teachers weren't going to tell us what was REALLY going on then it was up to us to find out ourselves.

And then Jodi got a REALLY SERIOUS look on her face and she said, "We need to make a plan to sneak into the STAFFROOM and

SPY ON THEM."

Spy Mission

Maisie didn't like the plan AT ALL. And she even took out her calculator and told us that the risk of getting caught was 99.999999999 per cent. And then she held up the calculator so we could all see.

But Jodi said that doing nothing WASN'T

AN OPTION and that in the WILD you have to

DO OR DIE.

And no one wanted to die so everyone agreed to do the plan.

We all stood outside the staffroom door and listened. Usually when we spy-listen on the teachers we hear loads of talking and laughing and one time we even heard a SCREAM. But this time all we could hear was the TV.

That's when Zach said, "I don't think there's anyone in there." But then we heard the sound of the kettle boiling so we knew there was at least one teacher in there.

Maisie started shaking a bit and saying that it was going to be IMPOSSIBLE to do the plan but then Jodi said that if we'd managed to hide in the school office under the office-ladies' desks when we thought there were BABY ALIENS at our school, then we could DEFINITELY sneak into the staffroom and hide behind the sofa.

Jodi said that we needed to create a

DIVERSION, which meant that we needed to do something to distract the teachers so they didn't notice us. And that's when I came up with a

BRILLIANT IDEA

and I know everyone else thought it was a brilliant idea too because I could see it in their EYES. I said that we should knock on the door and say that the scary DEPUTY HEAD TEACHER had asked to see them in her office and that they would all rush out RIGHT AWAY because they are even more scared of Mrs Seith than the pupils are. Then we could sneak in and wait for them all to come back. So Jodi looked at Zach because she thought that HE should be the one to knock on the door because she obviously didn't want to do it. And he just sighed and said fine because he is used to us making him do stuff like that.

So me and Jodi and Maisie all hid behind the big pot plant and held our breath as Zach knocked really loud three times.

Jodi looked MEGA ANNOYED and she hissed, "Why did you knock so loudly?! That's not what we discussed!" but Zach just

ignored her because he was in the middle of **THE PLAN** and also because Jodi **ALWAYS** likes to tell you how to do things, especially the things she doesn't want to do herself.

We all **STARED** at the door handle and waited for it to move. But it didn't.

Zach turned and looked at us and Jodi whispered, "Try it again." So he did. And he did it even **LOUDER** this time. But no one came.

So Zach came running back over to us and said, "We need a new plan."

But then Jodi got **THAT LOOK** and we all knew she had already come up with a new plan all by herself and that she was going to make us do it. She stood up and dusted off her knees and said, "WE'RE GOING IN!"

It took ages to pull Maisie out from behind the big pot plant because her hands were SO SWEATY that I couldn't get a proper grip on

them and also because she was doing that thing where you make your body go really heavy because you don't want to be picked up.

So I told Maisie that she should just stay there and be the lookout. But Maisie said that there was **NO WAY** she was staying there by herself and then she stopped making herself heavy and stood up.

So we all checked that no one was coming and then we **RAN** over and stood outside the staffroom door.

I held my breath as Jodi pulled down the door handle and opened the door a crack

and peeked inside. Then she whispered, "Clear," and started to walk inside so we followed her.

But then all of a sudden she

STOPPED DEAD

and I actually bumped right into her and Zach bumped into me but Maisie didn't bump into anyone because she'd run away.

I was just about to moan at Jodi because I'd hurt my toe on her foot when I saw why she'd stopped.

ALL of the teachers were in the staffroom

and they were ALL huddled around the TV.

Zach gasped and dropped to the ground and rolled behind one of the couches. And I was just about to do the same when I noticed that Jodi hadn't DROPPED AND ROLLED which is EXACTLY what she's taught us to do in these kind of situations.

Jodi was just standing there STARING at the teachers with her mouth WIDE OPEN.

So I grabbed her hand and pulled her down to the ground.

And **THAT'S** when we heard one of the teachers say, "I can't believe this is happening. This is a

NIGHTMARE."

And then another one said, "This is the worst thing that's ever happened

EVER."

The Eye of the Storm

Jodi made us stay behind the sofa for EXACTLY thirty seconds after the end-of-lunch bell had rung and all the teachers had left the room, and then she said,

"GO! GO! GO!"

and started to run.

So me and Zach ran after her. But Jodi kept running along the bottom corridor rather than going up the stairs towards our classroom which is the way we SHOULD have been going. So I shouted, "JODI!" but she couldn't hear me because she was too far ahead and she was weaving in and out of people because everyone was in the bottom corridor trying to get to their classes and nobody was lining up outside like normal and taking TURNS to come in because of the snow.

That's when Zach said, "She's leading us

back to The Den!"

But then before we could get much further I heard a little voice shout, "HELP!" and I turned and saw that Maisie had climbed on to one of the window sills to get away from all the people, and she looked TERRIFIED.

So I pushed my way through the crowd and stood underneath her and bent over a bit and shouted, "JUMP!" And she did because it is not the first time I have had to rescue Maisie by giving her a piggy back. And then we ran all the way to The Den.

When we got there Jodi was sitting on the ground with the door WIDE OPEN and she

was looking MEGA WEIRD.

So we rushed inside and shut the door and sat down.

And Zach said, "Jodi. PLEASE tell me where the bag of RATIONS is!"

Because he was freaking out a bit and wanted a biscuit to calm himself down.

Jodi just ignored him and said, "Did you hear it?"

But then Zach started asking about the biscuits again so I said, "SSSHHHHHH!" because I REALLY wanted to know what Jodi had heard in the staffroom.

And I said, "No. What did you hear, Jodi?"

And Jodi looked up at me and said,

"A BEAST IS COMING! IT'S COMING HERE!"

And we all GASPED.

Once we'd managed to get Maisie to stop screaming I said, "Jodi. Me and Zach were in there with you and we didn't hear anything about a beast."

And then Zach said, "Is this like the time you saw the goat?"

But then I gave Zach a LOOK and he stopped talking right away because, like I said, Jodi does not like to be reminded of that.

And that's when Jodi said, "It was on the TV."

And that made a bit more sense.

And Zach said, "What type of beast?"

And Jodi shrugged and said, "I don't know. It didn't say. I just heard the man on the TV say a BEAST is coming. And it's coming HERE."

And then Jodi looked at me and her eyes were HUGE. Usually Jodi does not look scared of ANYTHING but she looked scared of this.

I had

what was going on because I'd been SURE the TV man had been talking about the WEATHER and the SNOW. And Zach said he'd thought that too.

Maisie was nodding her head and agreeing with us loads because she was desperate for Jodi to be wrong about the BEAST.

That's when I remembered that Maisie hadn't been in the staffroom with us because she'd run away and she definitely hadn't seen Mr Beattie SOBBING in the corner.

So we told Maisie what had happened in the staffroom and she didn't say anything because she was too busy taking DEEP

BREATHS so she didn't faint again.

That's when Zach said that he heard the newsman say something about the SNOW STORM and a RED WARNING. And that he thought the teachers were in such a state because we were snowed in and the doors were probably frozen shut and there was a SUPER STORM headed RIGHT for our school.

Zach told us that he'd watched a documentary about SUPER STORMS. And then he went a bit quiet and looked at Maisie. But Maisie took a deep breath and nodded to him that it was fine to keep speaking and she made her BRAVE FACE.

So that's when Zach said that he was sorry to be the one to have to tell us that our lives were in DANGER and that was probably why the teachers were so upset.

Then he started saying loads of stuff like TORNADO OF SNOW and TWISTER and

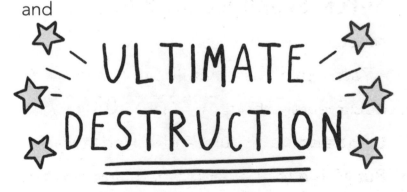

and Maisie's BRAVE FACE turned into her

FAINTING face because she had.

So we got the FAINTING BLANKET that we keep in the corner of The Den and wrapped her up tight so she would be warm while she had a little nap. Because there's not really much else you can do when Maisie faints of SHOCK so we just kept doing the SECRET MEETING.

Jodi said, "Should we not be EVACUATING?"

And Zach said, "Not if we're already TRAPPED."

I was really worried that the storm was headed directly for our school with us all trapped inside it. But I was also really worried that we were going to get into

MEGA TROUBLE

for being so late to class!

So I said that we should get to class but Jodi said, "No. We need to find out if this is true. And how much time we have to try to ESCAPE!"

And then she said that there was only ONE WAY to know for sure.

I gasped and Zach gulped because we both knew what Jodi meant. She meant we should sneak into the school office and SPY on the mega-scary OFFICE LADIES! Because the mega-scary OFFICE LADIES knew EVERYTHING!

Then before we could even discuss it, Jodi picked Maisie up in the blanket and threw her over her shoulder and said, "Let's go!"

The Beast from the East!

Jodi managed to carry Maisie all the way to the school reception without needing one of us to help her because Maisie is really small and also because Jodi said she'd had a **RUSH OF ADRENALIN** (which is a chemical your brain gives your body to make it strong when you are in a LIFE OR DEATH SITUATION).

When we got to the school office we saw that the door was WIDE OPEN and it is NEVER open. Not even a tiny crack!

Jodi said that the office ladies must have gone for their lunch and left the door open by mistake and that if the office was empty then this was the PERFECT OPPORTUNITY to sneak inside and hide.

I was NOT happy about that plan AT ALL because when we thought there were BABY ALIENS at our school I got stuck under one of the office-ladies' desks and she didn't know I was there and she kicked off her shoes and started wriggling her feet around and THAT'S when I saw her WEIRD ALIEN PINKY TOE that wasn't even really a toe and it didn't look like it had a nail on it.

But Jodi said that it was our ONLY CHANCE FOR SURVIVAL and then she ran into the office with Maisie and Zach. So I just took a deep breath and ran in too.

It was

SUPER CREEPY

in the office because it was COMPLETELY QUIET and EMPTY. And any time I have ever peeked in through the little glass window, it's always been full of office ladies, typing away at their computers and saying things loudly on the phone like

"UNACCEPTABLE" and "THAT IS NOT OUR PROBLEM" and "WHAT DID YOUR LAST SLAVE DIE OF?"

Jodi tried to pull Maisie under one of the desks but Maisie woke up and saw where she was. And I saw her open her mouth and I knew she was about to SCREAM THE WHOLE SCHOOL DOWN so I rushed forward and put my hand over her mouth. And even though she still screamed for ages you couldn't hear it as much because of my hand. And then she eventually stopped screaming and POINTED.

THAT'S when we saw that someone was

coming!

Jodi hissed, "HIDE!" and we all crawled under the desks.

Maisie GRIPPED my hand as we listened to the clip-clop footsteps getting CLOSER and CLOSER. Then the clip-clopping stopped because the person was INSIDE THE OFFICE and was standing on the carpet.

I held my breath and watched as the high heels walked past us.

And then we heard a SIGH and Maisie and I GASPED because we recognised that sigh.

It was Mrs Seith, the SCARY DEPUTY HEAD!

Then I saw that Jodi had started waving her arms about under the desk opposite and I realised that she was using a sign language called MAKATON that we'd learned in school (both Maisie and Jodi were really good at it and Maisie even went home and learned how to do more online).

Then Maisie turned to me and whispered, "Jodi says Mrs Seith is looking out of the window at something behind us." And then all of a sudden legs RACED past us and out the door and we heard really fast

clip-clopping because Mrs Seith had RUN AWAY.

Jodi got out from under the desk and ran over to see what Mrs Seith had been looking at.

And then she said, "It's safe. You can come out. The office ladies won't be coming back."

So we got out and I said, "How do you know that?"

And Jodi pointed to a note on the wall next to the photocopier that said

A LACK OF ORGANISATION ON YOUR PART DOES NOT CONSTITUTE AN EMERGENCY ON OURS.

I had **NO IDEA** what that meant so I looked at Maisie but she just shrugged so I knew that she didn't understand it either.

And then Jodi said, "Not THAT note. THAT note." And then she pointed to another note and it said,

WE HAVE GONE HOME.
WE ARE NOT WILLING
TO BE HERE WHEN
THE BEAST FROM THE
EAST ARRIVES.
OUR SAFETY COMES FIRST.

And Jodi said, "I KNEW THAT MAN SAID BEAST!"

And Zach said, "I can't believe there's a BEAST!"

And Maisie screamed the loudest I have ever heard a human scream.

And I didn't even try to stop her.

Because the

BEAST FROM THE EAST

was coming to OUR SCHOOL!

Who's TED?!

As soon as we got back to The Den we sat down and forced ourselves to drink a cup of cold tea because Zach said that his mum and gran ALWAYS have a cup of tea when they get bad news and that it helps.

So we all sat there drinking our tea but

it didn't really help me because it tasted horrible and Zach had burst the tea bag so I had loads of BITS floating in mine.

Then Jodi got up and turned over the bucket she had been sitting on and took out the FOOD RATION BAG and started eating a granola bar really quickly.

Zach said, "HEY! I thought we weren't allowed to do that!"

So Jodi just passed him the bag and didn't say anything and Zach didn't argue with that. He just grabbed a Mars Bar and ate it in two bites.

So I knew that meant we weren't doing

the food rationing any more and that it was probably because food was the LEAST of our problems now!

Zach said that the BEAST FROM THE EAST explained the teachers and the weeping and why it wasn't safe for us to go outside and why the school was open INDEFINITELY.

Then Maisie said, "What kind of BEAST do you think it is?"

And that's when Zach said he knew EXACTLY what type of beast it was.

Then he told us all to sit down and to hold hands for SUPPORT because what he was about to say was going to be HARD TO HEAR.

And it WAS hard to hear because as SOON as Zach opened his mouth someone shouted, "HELLO? HELLO?!" And it came from RIGHT outside The Den door!

Jodi's eyes almost POPPED out of her head because NO ONE is supposed to know about The Den! And the only other person in the whole entire school who knows is annoying Gary Petrie because he followed us one time. But we knew that it wasn't him because Jodi had WARNED HIM not to come to The Den OR ELSE and also

because the voice sounded like a woman's.

So we all froze. But then we heard, "HELLOOOOO? Can you hear me? Ted?"

And we all looked at each other because we had no idea who TED was.

And then the voice said, "Good. This is the only place I can get reception in this whole building."

We all sat in silence listening to whoever was on their mobile phone outside The Den talking to Ted.

And that's when we heard the voice say, "I'll never make it, Ted. Hello? Can you hear me? TED? I said THE BEAST FROM THE EAST HAS ARRIVED. I'LL NEVER MAKE IT. I'M SORRY."

Then we heard footsteps walk away so we knew that we were alone again.

And also that THE BEAST FROM THE

EAST HAD ARRIVED!

Then Zach gulped and said, "Are you ready for this?"

And Jodi said, "YES." And I nodded. But Maisie didn't do anything because she had wrapped her scarf around her WHOLE FACE because that is what she does sometimes when she can't handle what's going on.

And that's when Zach took a deep breath and said, "It's a

YETI."

I was VERY glad that Maisie had been

wearing the face scarf when Zach told us about the YETI because she screamed SO LOUD that I STILL had to cover my ears!

Jodi looked at me and I looked at her because even though almost TWO WHOLE MINUTES had passed since Zach told us about the YETI we were still both in a bit of SHOCK.

Because having a YETI loose in your school is TERRIFYING and I didn't know what YETIS liked to eat but I had a HORRIBLE feeling it might be US!

Maisie made a little gap in her face scarf for her mouth and she whimpered, "Not a YETI! Please. ANYTHING but a YETI!"

And I didn't know much about YETIS but I did NOT like how upset Maisie was getting about it because even though Maisie has had to deal with baby aliens, vampire rats and demon dinner ladies before, THIS was the most scared I'd ever seen her!

Jodi GRABBED the whiteboard and pen

and looked at Zach with her SERIOUS FACE and said, "We don't have much time. Tell me EVERYTHING you know about YETIS. Go!"

But Zach said that all he knew was that YETIS were HUGE BEASTS that live in the COLDEST PLACES ON EARTH because they have to live in SNOW to survive.

So Jodi said, "But how do we STOP ONE?!"

And Zach just sort of looked down at his shoes and didn't say anything. And Jodi said, "Oh," and then she looked down at her shoes too and I wasn't sure why everyone was looking down at their shoes and not speaking so I said, "Zach! How do you stop a YETI?"

And that's when Maisie said, "You don't." Then Maisie said that YETIS are

TOO BIG and

TOO STRONG and

TOO TERRIFYING

to stop.

And that's when Jodi got up and put her

coat on and said that we had to TRY and that there must be SOME WAY to stop a YETI and that we needed to find out MORE.

But Zach said that we didn't stand a CHANCE against a YETI and that it was TOO DANGEROUS to go outside and that we should just eat our RATIONS and LOCK ourselves inside The Den until the army came and CAPTURED the YETI.

And Maisie nodded her head LOADS. Or at least it looked like that was what she was doing because it was hard to tell with the scarf still wrapped around her head.

But then Jodi said that OBVIOUSLY the

127

army weren't coming because everyone was SNOWED IN and that it was UP TO US and that there was NO TIME TO PANIC.

And then she unwrapped Maisie's head and said, "Maisie. You know about YETIS, don't you?"

And Maisie nodded really slowly.

And Jodi said, "Did you read about them in the library?"

And Maisie nodded that she had and Jodi said that we needed to get to the library

ASAP

to find out more about YETIS.

But then Zach said that whoever had been outside the door had said that THE BEAST FROM THE EAST was HERE and that we couldn't be sure it hadn't SMASHED DOWN the school gates and wasn't loose in the playground by now.

So I said that that didn't matter because we were only going to the library and we weren't going outside. And AS SOON as I said it I remembered that the library isn't actually IN the school just now because the library is being REFURBISHED which means that we are getting an even BIGGER and

BETTER library and Mrs Bottery has set up a TEMPORARY library in a PORTACABIN in the playground.

Then Jodi said, "We need to get our hands on that book. It's our only chance of

SURVIVAL."

And then she stood up and started wrapping her scarf around her face, just like Maisie had and I knew Jodi wasn't making a face scarf because she was scared. She was making it because she was about to go out in a BLIZZARD.

And I knew that she was going to make us ALL go.

Even though there was a YETI loose in the playground!

BUCKle Up, People!

Jodi said that she was "PREPARED TO GO ALONE." And then she put her hands on her hips to show us that she MEANT IT.

But there was NO WAY I was going to let Jodi go by herself. So I wrapped my scarf around my face too, to show her I was

coming with her.

Then I looked at Zach and he looked up at the ceiling and tried to pretend that he didn't know I was looking at him. So I just KEPT ON LOOKING AT HIM and I made my eyes WIDER and WIDER and I didn't blink at ALL and then eventually he gave in and said, "FINE. I'll go."

So we made a PLAN and Jodi drew a MAP of the playground on the little whiteboard and said loads of stuff like,

"THIS IS A" and "THIS IS B" and "WE NEED TO GET FROM A TO B WITHOUT GETTING EATEN BY Y."

And that's when a little voice said, "I'm coming too."

We all STARED at Maisie because we were SHOCKED.

Then Maisie said, "I know which book we need and where to find it."

Zach said, "Are you sure?"

And Maisie took a deep breath and said, "Affirmative," and that made Jodi smile because that's what Jodi says you should say instead of YES when you are on a MISSION. And we WERE on a mission. A DANGEROUS mission. Because "A" (the school) and "B" (the portacabin) are actually REALLY FAR away from each other and we all knew that there weren't any trees or bushes or Year 6s to hide behind on our way across.

Jodi kept on pointing to the whiteboard and saying that we were **VULNERABLE TO ATTACK**, which meant that what we were doing was **MEGA RISKY**. And she looked at Maisie when she said it and Maisie didn't faint or **ANYTHING**.

Jodi said that as soon as we went through the Big Doors that there was **NO GOING BACK** and that we had to **HOLD HANDS** and **FORM A HUMAN CHAIN** so that we didn't lose anyone. And we all nodded.

Zach said that the temperature outside was

BELOW FREEZING and that we should wear WHATEVER WE COULD FIND on our way from here to the Big Doors and Jodi said that that was an EXCELLENT IDEA.

And then she said, "It's TIME!"

So we left The Den and started to make our way along the bottom corridor towards the Big Doors. And on the way we passed the Year 6 classroom and all of their coats and scarves were on the hanging rail in the corridor outside and Zach looked at Jodi and Jodi said, "DEFINITELY!"

So Zach started taking LOADS of scarfs and coats off the rail and then we all RAN

towards the Big Doors before anyone could spot us.

Once we reached the Big Doors me and Jodi and Zach put the stolen coats and scarves on over our own clothes. But Maisie didn't because she was already wearing two of her own coats AND a huge SNOW COAT that looked a bit like a giant, fluffy, duvet cover that had been made into a coat.

And that's when I realised something. Maisie's snow coat was WHITE.

So that's when I explained that we might not be able to SEE Maisie once we got outside because her coat was so big and so WHITE

that it was like SNOW CAMOUFLAGE.

And Zach GASPED and said that I was right and that it was lucky I'd noticed that now before we went outside otherwise WHO KNOWS what could have happened.

Zach said that he had an idea and he ran off and then came back two minutes later with a HUGE Post-it note block. I thought that he must have taken it from one of the classrooms without asking because none of our teachers let you have any of their Post-its (not even the yellow ones that no one likes) and I think it must be a rule or something that pupils aren't allowed them even though

I've never seen it written down anywhere and it **DEFINITELY** isn't on the

SCHOOL RULES

poster in our classroom.

But Zach said, "**ASK ME NO QUESTIONS.**" So we didn't. Then he said that his plan was to **COVER** Maisie in colourful Post-it notes so that we'd be able to see her in the snow. And that's when Jodi smiled.

Zach ripped the block into three smaller blocks and gave one to me and one to Jodi and told us to cover Maisie's white coat so that we'd be able to see her in the snow. So we did. And when we were finished it looked like Maisie had loads of colourful feathers like a tropical parrot or something!

And Maisie said that she LOVED IT and that if we made it out of this ALIVE she was probably going to do it to all her coats.

We were just about to form a HUMAN CHAIN and go out through the Big Doors when someone shouted, "HOLD IT RIGHT THERE!"

We GASPED and spun around and I was SURE it was going to be Mr Graves and that we were all going to get

EXPELLED

for not going to class AND for trying to go outside AND for stealing the Year 6s coats and blocks of Post-its!

But it WASN'T Mr Graves. It was annoying Gary Petrie!

And he said, "HA! You thought I was a teacher, didn't you?"

And we didn't say anything because when you speak back to Gary Petrie it just ENCOURAGES HIM to say something else and something else and SOMETHING ELSE and to be honest, we didn't have the time.

But then he noticed that we were wearing

all the coats and scarves and he said, "You're not going outside, aren't you?! You ARE. Aren't you?"

I just KNEW what the next thing out of Gary Petrie's mouth was going to be before he even SAID IT.

And I was right because he said, "I'm coming!"

And Jodi said, "No way!"

And Gary said, "WAY! Or I'm TELLING."

So Jodi said, "FINE! But you have to do EXACTLY what we say."

But Gary Petrie just smiled and we all knew that meant he WASN'T going to do exactly what Jodi said because that's what Gary is like.

So we all did the HUMAN CHAIN THING and Jodi pushed open the Big Doors with both hands.

And then she turned and looked at us and said, "Buckle up, people. LET'S DO THIS!"

Escape
from
Everest

As soon as we got outside Jodi said, "GO! GO! GO!" and we all held hands and ran towards the PORTACABIN LIBRARY because that was the plan.

It felt like it took AGES to get across the playground to the PORTACABIN LIBRARY even though we were running! And that was probably because the snow was DEEP and also because Maisie kept THROWING herself to the ground every time the wind made her Post-it notes flutter because she thought the noise was the YETI.

Then when we were almost at the cabin Gary said,

and Jodi got annoyed because it is usually Jodi who takes charge and tells us what to do and uses words like

Jodi said, "What is it?"

And that's when Gary said that he didn't actually know what we were doing or where we were going and also that he wanted to go back for his MONSTER MUNCH because he was hungry.

That's when Jodi said, "We don't have time for this! It's not SAFE out here!"

And Maisie said, "Gary. We can't go back to get your Monster Munch. There's a Beast from the East. We're going to the library to find out more. OK?"

But Gary didn't say anything back. He just STARED at Maisie with his mouth WIDE OPEN.

Then all of a sudden Zach said, "What's that?"

And he pointed to the ground. And that's when we saw the

HUGE

FOOTPRINT.

We all bent down and looked at it closely and we saw that there were little bits of HAIR around the edges of the footprint.

Then Gary said, "Um… That's a pretty big footprint. What KIND of beast are we talking about here?"

But we didn't even get a chance to answer because Jodi hissed, "Did you hear that?! GET DOWN!"

So we HIT THE DECK and listened closely but I couldn't hear anything because my heart was POUNDING. Then Jodi said that she'd heard a weird wailing sound off in the distance but it had stopped now.

So we all got up and kept moving through the snow as quickly as we could and when we reached the library cabin, Zach wiped the snow off one of the windows and peeked inside.

Then he turned to us and said, "The lights are off. Mrs Bottery isn't here."

And he put his hand on the door handle and pushed down. But the handle didn't move.

That's when I realised that the library cabin was LOCKED and that we were going to have to go back the way we came and risk getting EATEN by the YETI.

But then all of a sudden Maisie said, "Excuse me, please."

And then she reached forward and pressed 1234 into the little keypad above the handle and it WORKED! The door opened!

We all STARED at Maisie because what she had just done was actually

and we had no idea how she knew the code!

Gary said, "AWESOME!!"

And Maisie did a little smile and walked inside and we all followed her.

Once we were inside Jodi said that we should keep the lights off so that no one knew we were in there. And she gave me a bit of a SIDE LOOK when she said it and I knew that she'd meant that she didn't want the YETI to know we were in there but that she'd just said PEOPLE so that Maisie wouldn't freak out.

Then she said that Gary should stay at the window by the door and be the LOOK OUT.

And Gary said, "Is the BEAST really a YETI? That's so cool!"

And Jodi said that it WASN'T cool,

actually. And that it was actually

SERIOUSLY

DANGEROUS.

But Gary wasn't listening. He was too busy
STARING out the window, trying to see the
YETI.

We all watched as Maisie went behind
the librarian's desk and came back with a
REMOTE CONTROL. And then she pointed
it at the wall and pressed a button and hot
air started blowing down on us which was

good because my whole front was soaking wet from when Jodi had made us lie in the snow.

Maisie sat down on Mrs Bottery's seat and started tapping away on the computer.

I was a bit surprised at how well Maisie was COPING and how she was taking charge and I knew that it must be because she LOVES the library. And one time when Miss Jones told us to make a poster about our most favourite place in the whole world I remembered that Maisie had chosen the library.

And Maisie is actually the one who made

me join the library outside of school. And it's brilliant because I'm allowed to take out TEN BOOKS AT A TIME and I don't even have to pay or anything.

So anyway, we all went behind the desk too and watched as rows and rows of book information flashed in front of Maisie's eyes really quickly.

Maisie said that she was looking through the LIBRARY CATALOGUE to find out where the YETI book was.

And then she said, "GOT IT!" and she jumped down and disappeared behind a bookcase.

That's when Jodi grabbed me and Zach by the arm and whispered, "I definitely heard something out there!"

But then Maisie came back and Jodi let go of our arms and gave Maisie a little smile.

Maisie sat down on the floor and started flicking through a book called "EVEREST EXPLORERS" until she eventually stopped and said, "THERE!"

We all got down on the ground and looked at where Maisie was pointing and saw a picture of a man in the snow next to a

BIG FOOTPRINT.

That's when Maisie started reading aloud from the book and she said, "A photo taken of a possible YETI footprint near Mount Everest."

We all STARED at the photo and Zach said that it sort of looked like a human footprint would if the human wasn't wearing any socks

or shoes and was also a hairy giant. And I knew what he meant because you could see the pinky toe, and the big toe was

MASSIVE.

Jodi asked if there was anything else in the book about YETIS and then Maisie started reading out loads of stuff and this is what we found out:

THE YETI

Large ape-like creature

Covered in hair

Walks on two legs

Bigger than a human

Large hands and feet

Also called abominable snowman

There have been lots of YETI sightings near Mount Everest

Then Jodi said, "I think I know why everyone is calling the YETI the BEAST FROM THE EAST."

And then she got up and went to get an ATLAS (which is a book with all the maps of the whole world in it). Then she showed us one of the maps and pointed to ASIA and said that she remembered Miss Jones telling us that that was where Mount Everest was. And then she pointed to the four corners of the page and said,

"NEVER EAT SEA WEED"

(which is a WORD THING we use to remember what is NORTH, EAST, SOUTH and WEST). Then she said, "Asia is in the EAST! The BEAST FROM THE EAST!"

And that's when we found out that the YETI must have come all the way from Mount Everest to our playground.

Then Zach started reading from the book and that's when we found out that some people said that they smelled a STRONG SMELL just before a YETI SIGHTING and that some people believe that YETIS have a DISTINCT ODOUR (which means a terrible smell that only YETIS have).

Then he said, "It says here that in 1970 a British mountaineer was climbing in the Himalayas when he heard some odd high-pitched cries."

And AS SOON as Maisie read out that bit I looked at Jodi and her eyes were WIDE because she'd heard weird noises when we were running across the playground.

And then Maisie kept on reading and she said, "The next day he saw an ape-like creature looking for food."

That's when I noticed that Jodi had gone a bit pale.

Then Zach said, "Maybe that's the sound it

makes when it's

HUNGRY."

Then all of a sudden Jodi said she didn't feel very well and Zach shook his head and said that BAD NEWS was always HARD TO TAKE.

Maisie took a THERMOMETER out of her bag and started taking Jodi's temperature. But Jodi didn't have a temperature. She just had a sore tummy. So Maisie gave her some water and told her to lie in the RECOVERY POSITION. But Jodi said that there WASN'T TIME and she stood up and looked around at the portacabin.

Then she said, "We need to get out of here. I don't think this place is strong enough to keep a hungry YETI out."

And that's when Maisie said, "Where's Gary?"

And we looked and saw that Gary wasn't being the LOOK OUT any more and also that the door was WIDE OPEN.

We all RAN over to the door and looked outside but the blizzard was SO BAD we couldn't see a thing.

Then Maisie said, "Where did he go? Why

would he go out there on his own? What if the

YETI HAS HIM?!"

But we didn't know the answer to ANY of those questions.

So I said that he'd probably just gone back to school to get his Monster Munch and that calmed Maisie down a bit.

And that's when Jodi whispered to me and Zach that Gary was in GRAVE DANGER because THE EAST was a REALLY long way to travel from with no food. And Zach's eyes went WIDE and he nodded loads. And I gulped.

Because we were all thinking the same thing.

Gary might well have been hungry. But the YETI was

STARVING!

Post-it TORNADO!

When I walked out of the portacabin I knew that we were in DEEP TROUBLE because the snow was blowing and swirling EVERYWHERE.

Maisie was the last person in the HUMAN CHAIN and as SOON as she stepped outside, the blizzard blew ALL of the Post-it notes off her coat and made a sort of COLOURFUL TORNADO. And it was CHAOS!

Jodi was shouting at everyone to HOLD THE LINE because Zach had let go of Maisie's hand and was jumping around trying to catch the Post-its and I had let go of Jodi's hand so that I could get to Maisie because she was SHAKING VIOLENTLY and screaming. "IT'S A WHITE-OUT! IT'S A WHITE-OUT!" at the top of her lungs over and over.

And THAT'S when I heard something.

A weird WAILING SOUND!

I spun around but I couldn't see anything because of the blizzard. So I looked to see if Jodi had heard it and that's when I realised that I couldn't see Jodi or Zach any more! And it was IMPOSSIBLE to tell what was ground and what was sky because everything just looked COMPLETELY WHITE.

That's when Jodi yelled, "IZZY?"

And Maisie started shouting, "Is anyone there? IS ANYONE THERE?!" So I grabbed her hand and squeezed so she would know I was there – at least I thought it was her hand but its hard to tell with four pairs of gloves on.

And that's when Maisie screamed at the top of her lungs,

"THE YETI! IT'S HERE! IT JUST GRABBED MY NECK!"

After that it was TOTAL CHAOS.

Zach was screaming, "WHERE IS IT? I CAN'T SEE!"

And I was trying to tell him that it WASN'T a YETI that had touched Maisie's neck and

that it was ME. But he wasn't listening.

And Jodi was shouting, "HUMPBACK WHALE! HUMPBACK WHALE!" (because Humpback Whale is Maisie's CODE NAME that we use when things go SERIOUSLY WRONG).

But Maisie was GONE. She must have run away from me REALLY FAST and I knew

she could be MILES AWAY by now.

And that's when we all heard it.

A high-pitched YETI CRY!

And it sounded CLOSE.

So Jodi shouted, "RUN FOR YOUR LIFE!"

So we did.

As soon as we burst through the Big Doors to the school, Jodi yelled, "TOP FLOOR!"

And Zach yelled, "WE CAN'T LEAVE MAISIE OUT THERE!"

But Jodi said that we WEREN'T and that she left "NO MAN BEHIND" and then she ran up the stairs.

I had no idea what was going on and I was starting to PANIC because it really DID seem like we were leaving Maisie outside with a HUNGRY YETI! And we still didn't know if Gary had made it back safely or not!

But then Jodi yelled, "TRUST ME!"

And I looked at Zach and he looked at me

and I nodded because I know that Jodi is a
bit of an EXPERT in

EMERGENCY
SITUATIONS.

So we ran after Jodi and none of us stopped
until we reached the top floor.

I was EXHAUSTED when we got to the
top and I actually had to lie down on
the ground a bit and catch my breath.

That's when Zach said, "What's going on,
Jodi?"

And Jodi pointed out the window. And that's when we realised why Jodi had brought us up there. You could see the WHOLE PLAYGROUND FROM THE TOP FLOOR!

We all STARED out into the snow.

And Jodi said, "We probably won't be able to see Maisie because of her coat. So look for FOOTPRINTS."

And then Zach pointed at what looked like a bunch of footprints halfway between the cabin library and the school and said, "That's us! Look!"

And he was right because if you looked

really closely you could see the footprints coming back towards the Big Doors.

Then Zach said, "We need to get down to the next floor. I think I can see something!" And then he ran off. So we followed him and when we got there Zach pointed and said, "YES! LOOK! Tiny footprints!"

And that's when we saw a pair of tiny footprints going all the way from the bit where we had been standing to the OLD BIKE SHED!

And then I noticed ANOTHER pair of footprints near the library cabin that went out for a bit and then disappeared behind the cabin.

And I said, "LOOK! That must be Gary. He's still out there."

So Jodi said, "LET'S GO!"

But Zach said, "WAIT! Follow me!" and he ran off in the OPPOSITE direction and I had no idea where he was going and I wished everyone would stop saying "FOLLOW ME!" and then running off without actually saying where we were going!

So we followed Zach all the way to the gym and watched as he went into the store cupboard WITHOUT PERMISSION and came out with a GIANT NET.

And then he looked up at us with WIDE EYES and said,

"YETI TRAP!"

Then he ran back into the cupboard and came out with two badminton rackets and said that explorers in the book had had TENNIS RACKETS stuck to their shoes to make it easier to walk in the heavy snow but that we didn't have any tennis rackets since tennis got banned from our school after someone accidently hit a tennis ball at the head teacher's car and broke the little mirror

thing on the side.

But then Jodi said that the explorers in the book HADN'T had tennis rackets tied to their shoes and that that was RIDICULOUS.

So Zach said, "Oh really?"

And Jodi said, "Yes."

And Zach said, "Oh REALLY?"

And Jodi said, "YES!"

And Zach said, "OH REEEEEEEALLY?"

And I'd had ENOUGH of all this so I said, "Just show us, Zach!"

So Zach opened the book and pointed to the picture and Jodi didn't say anything after that because the explorers DID have tennis rackets tied to the bottom of their shoes so Zach was right.

Zach said that he needed some string to tie the rackets to his shoes but Jodi said that there wasn't TIME to look for STRING and then she opened her bag and brought out a roll of REALLY THICK Sellotape and said that Zach would just have to use that instead.

And before Jodi could zip her bag back up I saw that she had LOADS of stuff in there like a TORCH and the RATIONS BAG and I'm sure I saw a pair of HANDCUFFS.

So Zach took the Sellotape and then he put a foot on each badminton racket and wrapped the Sellotape round and round his foot until he could walk with the badminton rackets stuck to his feet.

Then he looked at us and said, "Your turn. Hurry!"

So we ran into the store cupboard and grabbed more badminton rackets and did the same. And I took three pairs of swimming goggles, too, to help us see in the BLIZZARD.

But it was really hard to walk because the long handles at the back kept hitting each other and I nearly fell over. But Zach said that it would be better once we got outside

in the snow and then he said, "Let's GO!"
and he tried to run like we usually do when
we do our missions and need to get places
FAST. But it didn't work this time because
he tripped and fell and we had to help get
him up.

Jodi stopped and put her hand on her stomach and I knew that she still wasn't feeling very well even though she wasn't saying anything and to be honest I was feeling a bit sick MYSELF because we were basically going on a

YETI EXPEDITION

in the playground!

So we all just walked REALLY CAREFULLY towards the Big Doors and Zach said that he thought we needed to

JUMP into the snow for the EXPLORER BADMINTON SHOES to work and to not get stuck because the snow was really thick on the ground now.

And then just as we got to the doors we heard FOOTSTEPS.

And we just KNEW that it was MRS SEITH,

THE SCARY DEPUTY HEAD,

because of the click-clicking sound her shoes make.

And that meant she was trying to TRACK US DOWN.

So Jodi pushed open the doors.

And we jumped out into the snow!

Badminton Racket Shoes

As soon as we got outside Zach yelled, "LOOK! IT'S WORKING!"

But I didn't really think it WAS working because we were having to walk more slowly than we did when we just had our boots on. And I knew that there was NO WAY we were going to be able to RUN if we saw the YETI.

The snow was still really thick so we kept on having to wipe our swimming goggles so we could see.

Jodi pointed ahead and said, "The bike shed's this way. Follow me! Stay as low to the ground as you can. And DON'T make any loud noises!"

And she looked right at Zach when she said it and I knew that she did that because of how LOUD he'd been when we'd first got outside and he'd got excited about his racket shoes.

So me and Zach followed and we crouched down as much as we could without falling over and followed Jodi all the way to the old bike shed. But when we got there Maisie was GONE. And that's when I spotted one of Maisie's mittens on the ground and I gasped and went completely still.

Because there was something next to it.

A big clump of

BROWN AND WHITE FUR.

And that's when we knew that we were too late.

The YETI had Maisie!

We all RAN outside again and looked around because we were PANICKING.

And then all of a sudden I smelled a REALLY BAD SMELL. And I GASPED because it was REALLY bad and also

because I knew it must be the

YETI'S DISTINCT ODOUR!

I turned around and looked at Zach because he was behind me and he said, "What?" But

I didn't say anything because I was worried that the YETI was CLOSE and that it would HEAR US if we made too much noise.

But then Zach's face CHANGED and I knew that he had

SMELLED THE SMELL

too! And when he put his hand up to his mouth and started making a choking sound I knew for SURE that he'd smelled it because it was HORRENDOUS and it was probably the worst smell I have ever smelled in my life.

And that's when I panicked a bit and I

shouted, "RUN!"

Zach sprinted ahead of me and I started to run after him, amazed at how fast he could run with the badminton shoes on.

But Jodi wouldn't budge. She was standing still, STARING at something.

And then she pointed and said, "Look!"

And I was panicking so I said, "Jodi! Can you not smell that?!

IT'S THE YETI!."

But Jodi gave me a weird look and said that she couldn't smell anything.

And then she said, "Izzy, look!"

Jodi was pointing at the

GIANT

SNOWMAN HEAD

Nola Burke had started making before Mr Graves had made us all go back into the school. Then Jodi said, "I think that's it. I think that's the YETI!"

So I wiped Jodi's goggles and told her it was just the giant snowman head.

But Jodi looked at me with WIDE EYES and said, "Are you SURE?"

So I said, "I'M SURE!"

Then I started to pull her after Zach and THAT'S when I saw it.

And Jodi said, "Did you see that?!"

And I was in SHOCK so I couldn't even ANSWER.

But I DID see it.

The snowman head was MOVING!!

And that's when I realised that it WASN'T a snowman at ALL.

It was the

YETI.

And it was COMING STRAIGHT FOR US!

I pulled off the badminton rackets and started screaming, and even though Jodi was waving her hands at me to stop, I couldn't.

So Jodi jumped on me and I fell to the ground and she put both hands over my mouth and said, "GET A HOLD OF YOURSELF! DO YOU WANT TO GET EATEN?!"

And that worked because I

DEFINITELY

didn't want to get eaten.

And that's when I heard it AGAIN. The WEIRD WAILING SOUND.

But it was MUCH louder this time.

Jodi was facing me and her eyes were **WIDE** and she said, "Whatever you do **DON'T** look behind you. Just

RUN!"

And I wished she hadn't said that because **AS SOON** as someone says that you just **HAVE** to look.

So I looked.

And that's the last thing I remember.

THE YETI BABY!

To this day I have **NO IDEA** how Jodi managed to carry me all the way back to the Big Doors and into the school. But she did.

As soon as Jodi laid me down on the corridor floor I woke up and Jodi said, "You're safe. Don't. Scream. You fainted.

When you saw. The YETI."

And it took her ages to say it because she was SERIOUSLY out of breath.

And that's when I remembered seeing the YETI coming at us in the playground and it had been TERRIFYING.

We both just lay there while Jodi caught her breath and that's when my brain came on again properly and I said, "ZACH!" because I'd just realised that we'd lost Zach now too!

And I was just thinking that of ALL the totally terrifying things we have had to deal with at this school we had NEVER lost THREE people at the same time before and

that this was SERIOUS.

Then all of a sudden I heard someone calling my name. And I looked at Jodi. And then we heard someone calling HER name, too.

So we sat up and we saw a small figure at the far end of the corridor and that's when Jodi said, "Uh oh. It's Mrs Seith. She's found us!"

And I knew that we'd probably get a detention in her office for not going to class because that is SERIOUSLY against the school rules. And I also knew that if we were in a detention we wouldn't be able to go back outside and save Maisie and Zach from the YETI.

So I said, "Run!"

But Jodi just STARED at me and it was obvious that she wasn't expecting me to say that we should run away from the deputy head teacher because her mouth was WIDE OPEN.

And then Mrs Seith must have heard me because she shouted, "Don't even THINK about it! You're in enough trouble as is it! I'll be calling your parents!"

And that's when we knew that there was NOTHING LEFT TO LOSE and that Mrs

Seith was going to call our parents anyway and that this was probably the most trouble we'd ever been in at school before and that we were definitely going to get

EXPELLED

this time.

So I started to run all the way up to the third floor and Jodi ran after me and once we got to the top she said, "You do realise that we're going to get expelled for life, don't you?"

And I said that I did and then we did a

quick pinky promise that we would make our mums send us to the same new school so that we wouldn't be on our own.

Then Jodi said, "We're lucky she wears those high heels. She'll never catch us."

But I knew that we still had to be quick because there might be other teachers looking for us too.

So we dropped to the ground and COMMANDO-CRAWLED along the corridor so the teachers wouldn't see us through the glass windows in the classroom doors and then we jumped up and looked out of the window at the playground.

That's when Jodi gasped and pointed and said, "THERE!"

And that's when I saw it.

And even though I tried not to, I SQUEALED a bit.

Because there was a

HUGE

HUNCHED BEAST

out there!

I stood with my mouth WIDE OPEN and watched as the YETI moved REALLY SLOWLY through the snow.

The YETI was covered in brown and

white hair and it looked like it was carrying something.

Jodi said, "I can't believe what I'm looking at. I can't believe this is REAL LIFE!"

And I couldn't believe it either because sometimes we are wrong about things but it was obvious that this time we were ABSOLUTELY RIGHT. Because there was a great big

in the playground!

Then Jodi said, "Why is it moving so

slowly?" And she pressed her face against the glass so she could see better and then she said, "Is that a BABY YETI?!"

And I looked carefully and noticed that whatever the YETI was carrying was white and FLUFFY.

And that's when Jodi said, "This is bad."

And I thought she meant that it was bad that there were TWO YETIS instead of just one. But then she said, "I'm pretty sure a MOTHER YETI is even MORE DANGEROUS than a normal YETI!"

Then Jodi explained that IN THE WILD mummy bears and gorillas and llamas will

do ANYTHING to PROTECT THEIR YOUNG and make sure they get FED.

But then all of a sudden Jodi gasped and said,

And I looked and saw that the YETI was even

to the school now.

And also that the baby YETI definitely

WASN'T a baby YETI.

Because baby YETIS don't wear red scarves.

But Maisie does!

Jodi started PANICKING and that is NOT NORMAL for Jodi so I knew that I had to BE STRONG and TAKE CHARGE.

So I grabbed Jodi by the face and said, "We're going to get her back. Do you hear me?"

But Jodi shook her head and said, "No. We're not. Did you see the way the YETI was holding her? It was holding her like a baby!

It thinks Maisie IS its baby! She'll never give her up."

And I realised that the YETI must have thought Maisie was a BABY YETI because she was wearing the FUR BOOTS and FLUFFY WHITE COAT and that BABY YETIS must have hairy feet and fluffy white fur like Maisie's coat.

Jodi leaned against the wall and sort of slumped down until she was sitting on the floor with her head in her hands.

But I wasn't ready to give up. And there was NO WAY I was going to let the YETI take Maisie.

So I grabbed Jodi and pulled her to her feet but then all of a sudden the swing doors BURST OPEN and we saw MRS SEITH standing there in her BARE FEET.

I froze on the spot and STARED AT HER because she was SWEATY and OUT OF BREATH and her hair had gone a bit WILD.

And I knew that she must have lost her shoes on the way up the stairs because it is quite a long way and that the heels on her shoes had maybe even BROKEN because of how many stairs there were.

I had NO IDEA what we were going to do because we were in

DEEP TROUBLE

for breaking the SCHOOL RULES and Mrs Seith was obviously RAGING about her shoes and she didn't even know that MAISIE HAD BEEN CAPTURED BY THE YETI!!

But then all of a sudden Mrs Akbar came RUNNING out of her classroom and gave Mrs Seith a great big hug and said, "We've been SAVED!!"

And I whispered, "RUN!" and we ran down the stairs faster than we have EVER run before and we both KNEW that we were

obviously **OFFICIALLY EXPELLED.**

But Jodi said that we had **BIGGER THINGS**

to worry about because Zach and Gary were

still LOST OUT THERE and also that she thought Mrs Akbar had said, "We've been SAVED!" because the ARMY were on their way with a tank and a helicopter and a huge STEEL CAGE for trapping the YETI before dropping it back on Mount Everest where it belonged.

So I started putting my badminton racket shoes back on but then Jodi kicked them away and said that we DIDN'T HAVE TIME and that I wasn't UNDERSTANDING and that we had to get to Maisie before the army did otherwise they would CAPTURE HER TOO. And I GASPED because I realised that the army would think Maisie was the YETI'S BABY and that she would get captured in the STEEL CAGE and dropped on MOUNT EVEREST TOO!

That's when Jodi pushed the Big Doors open and LOADS of snow blew in and Jodi had to actually HOLD ON to the door so she didn't get blown over.

And then she said, "We need to find Zach first. He's got the YETI NET. Are you ready for this, Izzy?"

And I knew that she was asking me if I was ready to TAKE ON A YETI. And I didn't think anyone was ever really READY to do that. But I knew that we didn't have a choice.

So I put my hand out and Jodi put her hand on top of mine and we said,

"LET'S DO THIS!"

And then I took a deep breath and we ran out into the snow.

ARE YOU IN THE BIN, GARY?!

I ran the fastest I have **EVER** run in my life and I fell about **TWENTY TIMES** but each time I just got up really quickly and kept on running.

Then all of a sudden Jodi stopped and I saw that we were at the recycling bins.

And Jodi said, "Gary. Are you in there?"

But we didn't hear anything back. So Jodi said it again a bit louder. But we still didn't hear anything.

But Jodi was CONVINCED that Gary was in the bins because she said that there wasn't anywhere else to hide in the playground and also that he was obsessed with them. So she made me lift her up so she could reach the lid and then she opened it and yelled, "ARE YOU IN THE BIN, GARY?!"

Jodi's yell ECHOED out of the bin and all around the playground.

And that's when I SMELLED THE SMELL.

And it was even STRONGER than it had been before so I knew that the YETI was CLOSE and that Jodi had LURED him to us with all her yelling into the bins!

That's when I said, "The bike shed!" because even though that obviously wasn't a very good place to hide from a YETI because that's where the YETI got Maisie, it was the only other place I could think of to look.

So we ran as fast as we could away from the smell and towards the old bike shed.

But it was EMPTY.

I looked down at where Maisie's mitten and the clump of fur were still lying in the

snow and I could feel myself getting MEGA UPSET.

Then all of a sudden we heard a THUMPING SOUND.

I froze and stared at Jodi.

Then we heard it AGAIN.

That's when Jodi looked up and whispered, "It's coming from the roof!"

I whispered back that we needed to

GET OUT OF THERE ASAP

because I thought that maybe the YETI had climbed up there and that the sound we were hearing was the sound a building makes before it COLLAPSES!

But then the thumping sound turned into a KNOCKING SOUND like when you knock at someone's door and you make a RAPPETY-TAP sound.

And Jodi looked at me with WIDE EYES and I said, "There's someone UP THERE!"

We ran out of the bike shed and looked up. But we couldn't see anything.

But then all of a sudden someone jumped down from the roof and landed in the snow and my heart almost LEAPT OUT OF MY BODY. That's how much of a fright I got!

I couldn't see who it was because they hadn't jumped very well and they'd landed FACE DOWN in the snow. But then the

person stood up and wiped the snow off and we saw that it was GARY!!

That's when Jodi said, "PLEASE tell me Zach's up there too??!"

But Gary just shook his head because he couldn't speak because his teeth were CHATTERING. And they were chattering so much that I thought he might have HYPOTHERMIA (which is when you get really ill because of the cold and Maisie always tells us that it is one of her mum's WORST FEARS FOR HER and that's why she makes Maisie wear AT LEAST three pairs of socks, even in July).

Gary was rubbing his hands together to keep warm and that's when I noticed that he didn't have any gloves on and also that his nose was BRIGHT RED. So I took my gloves off and gave them to Gary because even though he always has

CHEESY CRISP FINGERS

I didn't want them to FALL OFF because of FROSTBITE.

But Gary's hands were SO COLD that he couldn't even move them properly so I had to put the gloves on for him.

Then when Gary was eventually able to speak a bit he said, "Heard something behind cabin library. Went to look. Got lost in snow. So cold. So cold."

And then his teeth started chattering again so Jodi took off her scarf and wrapped it round his neck and said, "We have to get him back."

And then she lowered her voice a bit and said, "He might not have long."

And Gary must have heard because his eyes went WIDE and he tried to speak but Jodi just said, "SSSSHHHHHH!" and wrapped the scarf around his face and said,

"Save your energy for keeping WARM. Don't try to talk."

And then she gave me a bit of a LOOK and THAT'S when I realised that this was SERIOUS and that Gary Petrie definitely had HYPOTHERMIA.

So Jodi said that we were going to have to ABANDON trying to find Zach until we got Gary back and in an ambulance.

But then Gary managed to get his fingers working again and he unwrapped his face and said, "I'm fine! LOOK! I'm fine!"

And we looked and saw that his nose wasn't that red any more.

So then Jodi put her hand on Gary's head
and closed her eyes as if she was taking his
temperature with her hand and then Jodi
said he was

SAFE FOR NOW

but that she'd still need to keep an eye on
him.

And then Gary said, "I know where Zach
is."

And me and Jodi both gasped and said,
"WHERE?!" at EXACTLY the same time.

But Gary said that we wouldn't be able to
see Zach unless he showed us and that you

could only see him from the roof of the bike shed. And he didn't say anything annoying or make any of his annoying faces so we knew that he was SERIOUS.

So we climbed up the fence and on to the roof.

And as soon as we got up there Gary said, "LIE FLAT! Don't let it see you!"

So me and Jodi DROPPED DOWN FLAT and

COMMANDO-CRAWLED

to the edge of the roof so we could see.

And that's when Gary told us that he had been **YETI WATCHING** for a while and that he'd spotted it **FIVE TIMES**.

That's when Jodi said, "Where? What was it doing?"

And Gary said that he didn't know but it kept wandering **ALL OVER** the playground and that he thought it was stuck and couldn't find the way out.

But then Jodi said, "I think she knows **EXACTLY** where the way out is. She's not lost. She's **HUNGRY**. She probably **SMELLED YOU** but can't figure out where you are."

And Gary
GULPED and
then he pointed over to
the cabin library and said,
"Look. There!"

But we couldn't
see anything.

And then Gary said,
"The roof. Look at the ROOF."

And that's when we saw Zach.

And Jodi said, "He's ALIVE!"

And I STARED at her because I hadn't
realised that she thought Zach might not be
ALIVE!!

Then Jodi said, "Can he see us?"

And Gary said that he didn't think so and that he'd tried waving to him but that he hadn't waved back. Then Gary said that he'd been too scared to shout over in case the YETI heard him and came back.

Then all of a sudden Jodi said, "SHHHHHH! Do you hear that?"

That's when Jodi said that she thought she could hear the ARMY CHOPPER in the distance and that it was NOW OR NEVER. Which I knew meant we had to get Maisie back from the

YETI ASAP.

And that's when I SMELLED THE SMELL AGAIN.

And Gary held his nose and said, "YUCK! Who was that? Was that YOU, Izzy? It wasn't ME!!"

And I said that I KNEW it wasn't him and that it was the YETI and that it meant the YETI was CLOSE.

And then all of a sudden Gary gasped and grabbed my arm and whispered, "It's back!" And he pointed down to the ground.

And I almost SCREAMED because the YETI was RIGHT BELOW US!

We all STARED as the YETI made a GROANING sound and moved past us REALLY SLOWLY in the snow.

And then all of a sudden it stopped.

Jodi grabbed my hand and squeezed it tight.

And then Gary Petrie squeezed my other hand and I just let him because I was TERRIFIED.

Then Jodi whispered, "Does it still have Maisie?"

But I couldn't see anything except for the

YETI'S big hairy back!

Then Gary whispered, "Why has it stopped?"

But no one needed to answer that question.

Because that's when we all saw that Zach had finally spotted us.

And he was waving at us.

And jumping up and down.

And then he started YELLING AND WHISTLING!

And then all of a sudden the YETI started to move.

FAST.

And Jodi said, "Oh no!"

Because the YETI had spotted Zach.
And she was headed STRAIGHT FOR
HIM!

The YETI Trap!

Before I knew what I was doing I'd climbed down from the roof and was RACING across the playground.

And Jodi was running after me shouting, "ABORT MISSION! ABORT MISSION!" because she obviously wanted me to stop

but I COULDN'T.

The next thirty seconds were a bit of a BLUR but before I knew it I was at the CABIN LIBRARY and Zach was leaning over the roof looking down at me shouting, "IZZY! What are you DOING?! GRAB MY HAND!!"

I climbed up to the window ledge and Zach pulled me up on to the roof and I was in so much SHOCK that I had to lie down and just let the snow fall on my face for a second.

Then Zach said, "Why did you run over here like that? The YETI almost GOT YOU!"

And I felt a SHIVER go down my spine when Zach said that because even though I didn't remember running past the YETI I know that I must have. So I jumped up and told Zach that we needed to get out of there NOW and that the YETI was headed THIS WAY and that I'd come to SAVE HIM (even though I wasn't exactly sure how I was going to do that).

But Zach said that he KNEW the YETI was headed straight for him and that that was what he WANTED to happen and that that was why he'd been doing all the WAVING and YELLING and WHISTLING.

Then he started running around the roof touching things and pulling things and I had

what he was doing until he said, "You almost got caught in my YETI TRAP!"

And I GASPED when I saw what he had

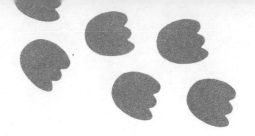

made.

Because Zach had attached the net to bits of ROPE and he'd tied loads of WEIRD KNOTS all over the place. It was AWESOME!

That's when Zach told me that he'd lost us after he SMELLED THE SMELL and that he was worried that the YETI had CAPTURED us so he ran back to the PE cupboard to get the ropes and dragged them all the way up here to make the TRAP.

I was AMAZED because the YETI trap looked really PROFESSIONAL and I had no idea Zach could do stuff like that.

Zach said, "I'm probably going to get

expelled for this."

So I said that me and Jodi were DEFINITELY getting expelled and I told him about Mrs Seith's broken heels and the BARE FEET and he looked SHOCKED.

And that's when I remembered that there was a YETI COMING TO EAT US so I rolled over on to my stomach and crawled to the edge of the roof to look for it.

But it was GONE.

I looked up and saw that Jodi and Gary were still on top of the old bike shed and that they were both waving at us LOADS and it looked like they were trying to tell us something.

Jodi was shouting something but the wind and snow were blowing SO HARD that I couldn't hear what it was.

I thought that maybe they were trying to tell us that the YETI was close. But I couldn't see it anywhere.

And that's when I realised that Jodi was using MAKATON again.

And I GASPED.

Because I knew what the sign she was doing meant.

Jodi was trying to tell us that the YETI was BEHIND US!

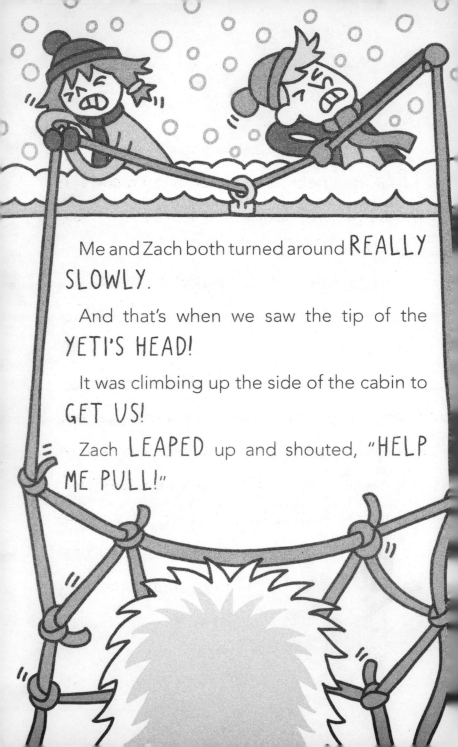

Me and Zach both turned around REALLY SLOWLY.

And that's when we saw the tip of the YETI'S HEAD!

It was climbing up the side of the cabin to GET US!

Zach LEAPED up and shouted, "HELP ME PULL!"

And I saw he was pulling on his YETI TRAP so I helped and then all of a sudden the YETI head disappeared and there was a LOUD GROAN.

And Zach yelled, "GOTCHA!"

And I couldn't believe it. We'd TRAPPED THE YETI!

So I yelled, "QUICK! Maisie might be stuck in the trap TOO! We need to get her out before the ARMY CHOPPER gets here and takes them both to Mount Everest!"

But Zach just STARED at me because he obviously had NO IDEA what I was talking about. And that's when I remembered that he didn't know about the whole MAISIE YETI BABY THING.

I looked over the side at the YETI to see if Maisie was trapped with it but it was hard to see because of all the THRASHING and the FUR.

So I climbed down and Zach said, "BE CAREFUL! Don't get too close!"

But I knew that I HAD to get close because if Maisie was stuck inside with the YETI then I was going to rip a little hole in the net to get her out.

But then all of a sudden the YETI stopped thrashing and started SCREAMING.

And I was surprised at how HUMAN a YETI CRY could sound.

And that's when I realised that I RECOGNISED the scream a bit. It sounded like MAISIE'S scream, only it was DEEPER and LOUDER.

I watched as the YETI kicked and screamed and

ITS FUR MOVED
AND I SAW
ITS FACE!

And that's when I realised that the YETI

WASN'T A YETI.

It was a

HUMAN
WOMAN.

And it wasn't just **ANY** human woman.

It was Maisie's mum!

Pink Bootlaces

Jodi came RACING over and I was just about to tell her that the YETI wasn't a YETI when she said, "IT'S NOT A YETI!"

And then Gary Petrie appeared and he was carrying Maisie and as SOON as she saw that we had caught her mum in a YETI

TRAP she started SCREAMING.

And that made Maisie's mum scream EVEN LOUDER.

And that's when I realised that we'd made a MASSIVE MISTAKE.

As soon as we managed to get some of Zach's SUPER KNOTS out, Maisie's mum RAN over to Maisie and gave her a great big hug (even though she was still covered in most of the net).

And she squeezed Maisie SO TIGHT that Maisie actually SQUEAKED.

Then Mr Graves appeared and he was FURIOUS and he said that he'd EVENTUALLY been able to find us because of all the SCREAMING and that we were in SERIOUS TROUBLE and that we needed to all get back inside NOW!

And then he spotted Maisie's mum and he

looked confused.

And he said, "Um. Mrs Miller? Is that YOU?"

And we knew that he probably didn't recognise her because of all the fur and snow and the giant net.

Once we were inside, Zach kept on apologising to Maisie's mum over and over again but she wasn't even listening because she was too busy putting Maisie into the RECOVERY POSITION. And she looked a bit like she was going to start CRYING. And I felt a bit like crying myself because it had been a SERIOUSLY STRESSFUL day and

I didn't really know what was going on or why Maisie's mum had dressed up as a YETI and been running around our playground.

Maisie's mum said that she hadn't meant to scare us and that she was just trying to get to Maisie to

SAVE HER FROM
THE SNOW.

And that's when we found out that her car had got stuck in the snow a mile from the school and that she'd had to WALK all the way here and that her legs and back were aching and that was why she'd been HUNCHED OVER and GROANING.

That's when Mr Graves ran and got Maisie's mum a chair and helped her to take her HUGE HAIRY COAT off. And I could see that he was a bit shocked that she had ANOTHER furry coat on underneath that one. And every time she took something off there was ANOTHER layer underneath.

Then Maisie's mum said, "I tried to come in through the front gates but they were locked. I pressed the buzzer but no one from the office answered."

And I looked at Jodi because we knew that the office ladies had gone home early.

And then she said, "So I came round the back and tried to walk through the playground to get in that way. And that's when I heard my little

screaming!"

That's when Maisie told us that her mum had found her in the old bike shed after she'd run away from us and that her mum had carried her all the way back to the school.

Then Maisie's mum said, "I came back to try to rescue the rest of you because Maisie said you were still out there!"

That's when Jodi said that as soon as I'd jumped down from the bike shed to save Zach she'd noticed something odd about the YETI'S feet. And that's when I looked at Maisie's mum's feet and saw that she was wearing the same FURRY BOOTS as Maisie and that her boots had PINK STRAPS.

Jodi said that that's when she realised that it WASN'T a YETI because YETIS don't have pink laces in their boot, or any boots at all! And that it was just Maisie's mum wearing a HUGE hairy coat.

And that's when I realised that the fur we'd found next to Maisie's mitten must have come from her mum's coat.

Jodi said that was why she'd shouted, "ABORT MISSION!"

So I said, "But I saw you signing with Makaton. You said,

LOOK BEHIND YOU!"

But Jodi said that she DIDN'T and that

she'd been signing the word "STOP!" over and over and that's when I realised that I was even WORSE at Makaton that I thought I was.

Then Gary said, "So what was that horrible SMELL? Izzy said it was the YETI."

And that's when Jodi's face went BRIGHT RED and she looked down at the ground and said, "It was me. I think it's the beans. They must be out of date. I'm sorry."

And that's when I remembered about Jodi's SORE STOMACH and how she'd gone up for THIRDS AND FOURTHS of the WAR BEANS!

And I looked at Jodi with my mouth WIDE OPEN because I couldn't BELIEVE that she didn't say anything before now, and I'm not saying what happened was all her fault or anything, but she DEFINITELY should have told us that the smell was coming from HER and not the YETI!!

But Jodi just looked away and said, "So what's going on? Is there still a BEAST FROM THE EAST headed this way?"

And Mr Graves looked a bit confused for a minute and then he smiled and said, "Ah. I think I know what's happened here. Who told you about the Beast from the East?"

And we just looked at each other and didn't say anything because we didn't want to admit that we'd caused a DIVERSION and sneaked into the staffroom and

SPIED

on all the teachers because we knew that we were ALREADY IN ENOUGH TROUBLE.

So that's when Mr Graves explained that the Beast from the East wasn't actually a BEAST and that it was a TERRIBLE SNOW STORM that people had just NICKNAMED the Beast from the East.

Mr Graves said that the storm had started in Russia and come all the way to Scotland and that there was a RED WEATHER WARNING and that it wasn't safe to travel and that lots of cars and vans, buses and trains had got stuck in the snow. But the good news was that they'd heard on the radio not

long ago that the storm was CALMING and that the roads would be cleared and that the buses would be back on by this evening.

So I asked Mr Graves why all the teachers had been so UPSET and why Mr Beattie and some of the other teachers had been crying if our lives hadn't been at risk after all.

And that's when Mr Graves coughed and said that it was because the teachers worked REALLY HARD and that they were just a bit upset that they had to stay at school for an extra couple of hours after a LONG WEEK.

And I looked at Jodi and she looked at me

because that didn't really make any sense because **WE'D** been here all week too but we didn't start crying when we found out we had to stay for an extra couple of hours!

But then Zach said, "So what was making the **WEIRD WAILING** sound?"

And that's when Maisie's mum started hugging Maisie really tightly again and she said, "That was me. I was just **SO WORRIED** about my **LITTLE LAMB!** I couldn't stop **CRYING!**"

Mr Graves put his hand on Maisie's mum's shoulder and apologised over and over for not being able to keep us inside the school

where we should have been.

And then he gave us all a bit of a LOOK and we all knew that that meant we were getting

But Maisie's mum wasn't really listening to Mr Graves because she was too busy taking Maisie's PULSE.

I was a bit annoyed at the LOOK Mr Graves had given us because everything wasn't just OUR fault. And it had been Maisie's mum who had been the one running around the playground dressed as a YETI! And I was about to say that when Mrs Seith appeared and I knew that this was IT and that she was probably about to take four letters out of her pocket that said:

EXPELLED FOR LIFE
FROM ST VINCENT'S
PRIMARY SCHOOL.

But she didn't.

She said, "If it's OK with you, Mr Graves, I'll be going home now."

And we all saw that she was only wearing

one shoe. But nobody said anything. And as soon as Mr Graves said yes, Mrs Seith did a little smile and RAN out of the school. She even buried straight through the snowdrift blocking the gates. And I watched her for ages because she looked funny going up and down and up and down because she only had one heel and I knew that she must be desperate to get home and get a new pair of high heels on because she obviously loves wearing them so much.

Jodi looked at me and smiled a HUGE SMILE because she was thinking the same thing as me and that we had GOT AWAY with not going to class AND with stealing the Year 6 coats AND with taking the Post-its and the big net and all the rope without permission AND for going outside on a YETI MISSION when we were supposed to be in class.

Then Zach said, "Can we go home now, too?"

And Mr Graves said, "Not quite yet. Most of the cars in the car park are still buried in the snow and the entrance to the school is still blocked with snow. And we don't seem to have a shovel anywhere."

And that's when Maisie's mum LEAPED up, put her big hairy coat back on and rushed out into the snow.

And when she came back she had a HUGE BACKPACK with her and there was loads of stuff strapped to it like a massive PILLOW and a FRYING PAN and a SHOVEL.

Maisie's mum said that she brought "EVERYTHING THAT SHE COULD" as

SOON as she heard about the school and the snow.

And then she gave the shovel to Mr Graves and he said thank you.

But then he just sort of stood there so we asked him if he was OK and he said that he was fine but that he didn't actually have a COAT with him and that he'd only worn his SUIT JACKET to work.

So Maisie's mum took off her

YETI COAT

and put it over Mr Graves's shoulders and said, "There you go."

And we all watched from the window as

Mr Graves dug all the cars out of the snow and cleared the entrance. And Maisie's mum said, "Oh GOODNESS! That coat really DOES make him look like a YETI, doesn't it? Poor LAMBS. You must have all been

of me!"

And then she started giggling a bit. And then she started giggling a LOT.

And then Maisie said, "Mum. You WERE making some weird animal noises. Especially when Zach caught you in the YETI trap."

And that made Maisie's mum giggle even MORE. And then she made a YETI NOISE and we all BURST OUT LAUGHING just as the first school bus rolled through the gate.

Acknowledgements

Thank you to baby Albie for letting Mummy write this book during your nap time. Knowing you could wake at ANY SECOND has made this the most frantic Izzy adventure yet!

Thanks also to the dream team that is Tom and Nicola for the YETILICIOUS design and illustrations. You've done it again! It's my new totally favourite cover!

And a huge, huggy thank you to my editor, Kirsty, for her "Maisie's mum in the playground" suggestion (pure genius!). Love and pugs 4eva!

Being on book tour with my 10-week-old during "The Beast from the East" snowstorm inspired this book. So, I guess I'd like to say thanks to the Beast (trapping us in a train for ten hours gave me plenty of time to plot the book!).

And a huge THANK YOU to all the Crows and my agent, Becky, for going above-and-beyond during that snowy tour. I feel very lucky to have you all in my life. Thank you.

A special thanks goes out to Catherine Stokes (aka "Legs of Steel") for taking on the Beast with her super-powerful high kick, rescuing me, baby and husband, and an entire carriage of train passengers. (That frozen door didn't stand a CHANCE!)

Finally, I'd like to thank my husband, Andy, for his love and support. Never has one man made so many Sainsbury's trips for coconut water and Danish pastries.